Dear Parent:

Congratulations! Your child is taking
the first steps on an exciting journey.
The destination? Independent reading!

STEP INTO READING® will help your child get there. The program offers
five steps to reading success. Each step includes fun stories and colorful art.
There are also Step into Reading Sticker Books, Step into Reading Math
Readers, Step into Reading Phonics Readers, Step into Reading Write-In
Readers, and Step into Reading Phonics Boxed Sets—a complete literacy
program with something to interest every child.

Learning to Read, Step by Step!

Ready to Read   Preschool–Kindergarten
• big type and easy words • rhyme and rhythm • picture clues
For children who know the alphabet and are eager to
begin reading.

Reading with Help   Preschool–Grade 1
• basic vocabulary • short sentences • simple stories
For children who recognize familiar words and sound out
new words with help.

Reading on Your Own   Grades 1–3
• engaging characters • easy-to-follow plots • popular topics
For children who are ready to read on their own.

Reading Paragraphs   Grades 2–3
• challenging vocabulary • short paragraphs • exciting stories
For newly independent readers who read simple sentences
with confidence.

Ready for Chapters   Grades 2–4
• chapters • longer paragraphs • full-color art
For children who want to take the plunge into chapter books
but still like colorful pictures.

STEP INTO READING® is designed to give every child a successful
reading experience. The grade levels are only guides. Children can progress
through the steps at their own speed, developing confidence in their
reading, no matter what their grade.

Remember, a lifetime love of reading starts with a single step!

Thomas the Tank Engine & Friends™

CREATED BY BRITT ALLCROFT

Based on The Railway Series by The Reverend W Awdry.
© 2010 Gullane (Thomas) LLC.
Thomas the Tank Engine & Friends and Thomas & Friends are trademarks of Gullane (Thomas) Limited.

HIT and the HIT Entertainment logo are trademarks of HIT Entertainment Limited.

Visit us on the Web!
StepIntoReading.com
www.randomhouse.com/kids
www.thomasandfriends.com

Educators and librarians, for a variety of teaching tools,
visit us at www.randomhouse.com/teachers

Library of Congress Cataloging-in-Publication Data
Trouble in the tunnel / illustrated by Richard Courtney. — 1st ed.
    p. cm. — (Step into reading)
"Based on The Railway Series by The Reverend W. Awdry."
"Thomas the Tank Engine & Friends created by Britt Allcroft."
ISBN 978-0-375-86696-8 (trade) — ISBN 978-0-375-96696-5 (lib. bdg.)
I. Courtney, Richard, ill. II. Awdry, W. Railway series.
III. Thomas the tank engine and friends.
PZ7.T5335 2010
[E]—dc22   2010005871

Printed in the United States of America
10 9 8 7 6 5 4 3 2 1

HIT entertainment

TROUBLE IN THE TUNNEL

Based on The Railway Series
by the Reverend W Awdry

Illustrated by Richard Courtney

Random House New York

Peep! Peep!

Thomas was going
to the Mainland.
Cranky lifted him
onto a raft.
"Goodbye!" called Thomas.

The boat sailed to sea.

Thomas bobbed
behind on the raft.

Soon night came.

Thomas could not see.

But he could hear.

Crack! Crash!

The chain snapped.

"Help!" cried Thomas.

The boat
chugged away.
Thomas was all alone.
Thomas was scared!

The next morning,
the raft floated
to a far-off island.

How would Thomas find
his way back to Sodor?

Clickety-clack.

Thomas rattled
around a bend.

Then—*screech!*

He stopped.

Three strange engines
were in front of him!

"I'm Bash," said one.

"I'm Dash,"
said another.

"I'm Ferdinand,"
peeped the last.

The new engines said
they could help Thomas.
But they were silly.
They made jokes.
They teased Thomas.

He huffed away.

He puffed up hills.

He chuffed past rocks.

He raced along the track.

Thomas was lost.

Now he *needed* help!

Thomas found Bash,
Dash, and Ferdinand.
"I need help,"
said Thomas.
"Will you tell me
how to get home?"

The engines took Thomas
to an old tunnel.
"This leads to Sodor,"
they said.

They puffed inside.
The tunnel was dark.
The tracks were twisty.

Smash! Crash!

Rocks tumbled down.
Thomas and the engines
were stuck!

The engines had a plan.
They told Thomas to
puff as hard as he could.
Puff-puff-puff!
Thomas' puffs rose
high into the sky.

Back on Sodor,
Percy wondered
where Thomas was.

Then he saw three puffs!

"Thomas!" cried Percy.

He whooshed away

to get help.

Clickety-clack.

Clickety-clack.

Thomas heard something
in the tunnel.

"We'll save you!"

peeped Percy.

The engines from Sodor

bashed through the rocks.

Thomas was rescued.
Hooray!